Martians, Keep Out!

THE MOON
THAT VANISHED

by Leigh Brackett

DOWN TO THE DARKLING SEA

The stranger was talking about him—the tall stranger who was a long way from his native uplands, who wore plain leather and did not belong in this swamp-coast village. He was asking questions, talking, watching.

David Heath knew that, in the same detached way in which he realized that he was in Kalruna's dingy Palace of All Possible Delights, that he was very drunk but not nearly drunk enough, that he would never be drunk enough and that presently, when he passed out, he would be tossed over the back railing into the mud, where he might drown or sleep it off as he pleased.

Heath did not care. The dead and the mad do not care. He lay without moving on the native hide-frame cot, the leather mask covering the lower part of his face, and breathed the warm golden vapour that bubbled in a narghil-like bowl beside him. Breathed, and tried to sleep, and could not. He did not close his eyes. Only when he became unconscious would he do that.

There would be a moment he could not avoid, just before his drugged brain slipped over the edge into oblivion, when he would no longer be able to see anything but the haunted darkness of his own mind, and that moment would seem like all eternity. But afterward, for a few hours, he would find peace.

Until then he would watch, from his dark corner, the life that went on in the Palace of All Possible Delights.

Heath rolled his head slightly. By his shoulder, clinging with its hooked claws to the cot frame, a little bright-scaled dragon crouched and met his glance with jewel-red eyes in which there were peculiar sympathy and intelligence. Heath smiled and settled back. A nervous spasm shook him but the drug had relaxed him so that it was not severe and passed off quickly.

No one came near him except the emerald-skinned girl from the deep swamps who replenished his bowl. She was not human and therefore did not mind that he was David Heath. It was as though there were a wall around him beyond which no man stepped or looked.

Except, of course, the stranger.

Heath let his gaze wander. Past the long low bar where the common seamen lay on cushions of moss and skins, drinking the cheap fiery *thul*. Past the tables, where the captains and the mates sat, playing their endless and complicated dice games. Past the Nahali girl who danced naked in the torchlight, her body glimmering with tiny scales and as sinuous and silent in motion as the body of a snake.

The single huge room was open on three sides to the steaming night. It was there that Heath's gaze went at last. Outside, to the darkness and the sea, because they had been his life and he loved them.

THE MOON THAT VANISHED

Darkness on Venus is not like the darkness of Earth or Mars. The planet is hungry for light and will not let it go. The face of Venus never sees the sun but even at night the hope and the memory of it are there, trapped in the eternal clouds.

The air is the colour of indigo and it carries its own pale glow. Heath lay watching how the slow hot wind made drifts of light among the *liha*-trees, touched the muddy harbour beaches with a wavering gleam and blended into the restless phosphorescence of the Sea of Morning Opals. Half a mile south the river Omaz flowed silently down, still tainted with the reek of the Deep Swamps.

Sea and sky—the life of David Heath and his destruction.

The heavy vapor swirled in Heath's brain. His breathing slowed and deepened. His lids grew heavy.

Heath closed his eyes.

An expression of excitement, of yearning, crossed his face, mingled with a vague unease. His muscles tensed. He began to whimper, very softly, the sound muffled by the leather mask.

The little dragon cocked its head and watched, still as a carven image.

*

Heath's body, half naked in a native kilt, began to twitch, then to move in spasmodic jerks. The expression of unease deepened, changed gradually to one of pure horror. The cords in his throat stood out like wires as he tried to cry out and could not. Sweat gathered in great beads on his skin.

Suddenly the little dragon raised its wings and voiced a hissing scream.

Heath's nightmare world rocked around him, riven with loud sounds. He was mad with fear, he was dying, vast striding shapes thronged toward him out of a shining mist. His body was shaken, cracking, frail bones bursting into powder, his heart tearing out of him, his brain a part of the mist, shining burning. He tore the mask from his face and cried out a name, *Ethne!*, and sat up—and his eyes were wide open, blind and deep.

Somewhere, far off, he heard thunder. The thunder spoke. It called his name. A new face pushed in past the phantoms of his dream. It swelled and blotted out the others. The face of the stranger from the High Plateaus. He saw every line of it, painted in fire upon his brain.

The square jaw, hard mouth, nose curved like a falcon's beak, the scars wealed white against white skin, eyes like moonstones, only hot, bright—the long silver hair piled high in the intricate tribal knot and secured with a warrior's golden chains.

Hands shook him, slapped his face. The little dragon went on screaming and flapping, tethered by a short thong to the head of Heath's cot so that it could not tear out the eyes of the stranger.

Heath caught his breath in a long shuddering sob and sprang.

He would have killed the man who had robbed him of his little time of peace. He tried, in deadly silence, while the seamen and the masters and the mates and the dancing girls watched, not moving, sidelong out of their frightened, hateful eyes. But the Uplander was a big man, bigger than Heath in his best days had even been. And presently Heath lay panting on the cot, a sick man, a man who was slowly dying and had no strength left.

The stranger spoke. "It is said that you found the Moonfire."

Heath stared at him with his dazed, drugged eyes and did not answer.

"It is said that you are David Heath the Earthman, captain of the *Ethne*."

Still Heath did not answer. The rusty torchlight flickered over him, painting highlight and shadow. He had always been a lean, wiry man. Now he was emaciated, the bones of his face showing terribly ridged and curved under the drawn skin. His black hair and unkempt beard were shot through with white.

The Uplander studied Heath deliberately, contemptuously. He said, "I think they lie."

Heath laughed. It was not a nice laugh.

"Few men have ever reached the Moonfire," the Venusian said. "They were the strong ones, the men without fear."

After a long while Heath whispered, "They were fools."

He was not speaking to the Uplander. He had forgotten him. His dark mad gaze was fixed on something only he could see.

"Their ships are rotting in the weed-beds of the Upper Seas. The little dragons have picked their bones." Heath's voice was slow, harsh and toneless, wandering. "Beyond the Sea of Morning Opals, beyond the weeds and the Guardians, through the Dragon's Throat and still beyond—I've seen it, rising out of the mists, out of the Ocean-That-Is-Not-Water."

A tremor shook him, twisting the gaunt bones of his body. He lifted his head, like a man straining to breathe, and the running torchlight brought his face clear of the shadows. In all the huge room there was not a sound, not a rustle, except for a small sharp gasp that ran through every mouth and then was silent.

"The gods know where they are now, the strong brave men who went through the

Moonfire. The gods know what they are now. Not human if they live at all."

He stopped. A deep slow shudder went through him. He dropped his head. "I was only in the fringe of it. Only a little way."

In the utter quiet the Uplander laughed. He said, "I think you lie."

Heath did not raise his head nor move. The Venusian leaned over him, speaking loudly, so that even across the distance of drugs and madness the Earthman should hear.

"You're like the others, the few who have come back. But they never lived a season out. They died or killed themselves. How long have you lived?"

*

Presently he grasped the Earthman's shoulder and shook it roughly. "How long have you lived?" he shouted and the little dragon screamed, struggling against its thong.

Heath moaned. "Through all hell," he whispered. "Forever."

"Three seasons," said the Venusian. "Three seasons, and part of a fourth." He took his hand away from Heath and stepped back. "You never saw the Moonfire. You knew the custom, how the men who break the tabu must be treated until the punishment of the gods is finished."

He kicked the bowl, breaking it, and the bubbling golden fluid spilled out across the floor in a pool of heady fragrance. "You wanted *that*, and you knew how to get it, for the rest of your sodden life."

A low growl of anger rose in the Palace of All Possible Delights.

Heath's blurred vision made out the squat fat bulk of Kalruna approaching. Even in the depths of his agony he laughed, weakly. For more than three seasons Kalruna had obeyed the traditional law. He had fed and made drunk the pariah who was sacred to the anger of the gods—the gods who guarded so jealously the secret of the Moonfire. Now Kalruna was full of doubt and very angry.

Heath began to laugh aloud. The effects of his uncompleted jag were making him reckless and hysterical. He sat up on the cot and laughed in their faces.

"I was only in the fringe," he said. "I'm not a god. I'm not even a man any more. But I can show you if you want to be shown."

He pulled himself to his feet, and as he did so, in a motion as automatic as breathing, he loosed the little dragon and set it on his naked shoulder. He stood swaying a moment and then began to walk out across the room, slowly, uncertainly, but with his head stubbornly erect. The crowd drew apart to make a path for him and he walked along it in the silence, clothed in his few sad rags of dignity, until he came to the railing and stopped.

"Put out the torches," he said. "All but one."

Kalruna said hesitantly, "There's no need. I believe you."

There was fear in the place now—fear, and fascination. Every man glanced sideways, looking for escape, but no one went away.

Heath said again, "Put out the torches."

The tall stranger reached out and doused the nearest one in its bucket, and presently in all that vast room there was darkness, except for one torch far in the back.

Heath stood braced against the rail, staring out into the hot indigo night.

The mists rose thick from the Sea of Morning Opals. They crept up out of the mud, and breathed in clouds from the swamps. The slow wind pushed them in long rolling drifts, blue-white and glimmering against the darker night.

Heath looked hungrily into the mists. His head was thrown back, his whole body strained upward and presently he raised his arms in a gesture of terrible longing.

"Ethne," he whispered. "Ethne."

Almost imperceptibly, a change came over him. The weakness, the look of the sodden wreck, left him. He stood firm and straight, and the muscles rose coiled and beautiful on the long lean frame of his bones, alive with the tension of strength.

His face had altered even more. There was a look of power on it. The dark eyes burned with deep fires, glowing with a light that was more than human, until it seemed that his whole head was crowned with a strange nimbus.

For one short moment, the face of David Heath was the face of a god.

"Ethne," he said.

And she came.

Out of the blue darkness, out of the mist, drifting tenuous and lovely toward the Earthman. Her body was made from the glowing air, the soft drops of the mist, shaped and coloured by the force that was in Heath. She was young, not more than nineteen, with the rosy tint of Earth's sun still in her cheeks, her eyes wide and bright as a child's, her body slim with the sweet angularity of youth.

The first time I saw her, when she stepped down the loading ramp for her first look at Venus and the wind took her hair and played with it and she walked light and eager as a colt on a spring morning. Light and merry always, even walking to her death.

The shadowy figure smiled and held out her arms. Her face was the face of a woman who has found love and all the world along with it.

Closer and closer she drifted to Heath and the Earthman stretched out his hands to touch her.

And in one swift instant, she was gone.

Heath fell forward against the rail. He stayed there a long time. There was no god in him now, no strength. He was like a flame suddenly burned out and dead, the ashes collapsing upon themselves. His eyes were closed and tears ran out from under the lashes.

*

In the steaming darkness of the room no one moved.

Heath spoke once. "I couldn't go far enough," he said, "into the Moonfire."

He dragged himself upright after a while and went toward the steps, supporting himself against the rail, feeling his way like a blind man. He went down the four steps of hewn logs and the mud of the path rose warm around his ankles. He passed between the rows of mud-and-wattle huts, a broken scarecrow of a man plodding through the night of an alien world.

He turned, down the side path that led to the anchorage. His feet slipped into the deeper mud at the side and he fell, face down. He tried once to get up, then lay still, already sinking into the black, rich ooze. The little dragon rode on his shoulder, pecking at him, screaming, but he did not hear.

He did not know it when the tall stranger from the High Plateaus picked him out of the mud a few seconds later, dragon and all, and carried him away, down to the darkling sea.

THE EMERALD SAIL

A woman's voice said, "Give me the cup."

Heath felt his head being lifted, and then the black, stinging taste of Venusian coffee slid like liquid fire down his throat. He made his usual waking fight against fear and reality, gasped and opened his eyes.

He lay in his own bunk, in his own cabin, aboard the *Ethne*. Across from him, crouched on a carven chest, the tall Venusian sat, his head bowed under the low scarlet arch of the deck above. Beside Heath, looking down at him, was a woman.

It was still night. The mud that clung to Heath's body was still wet. They must have worked hard, he thought, to bring him to.

10

The little dragon flopped down to its perch on Heath's shoulder. He stroked its scaly neck and lay watching his visitors.

The man said, "Can you talk now?"

Heath shrugged. His eyes were on the woman. She was tall but not too tall, young but not too young. Her body was everything a woman's body ought to be, of its type, which was wide-shouldered and leggy, and she had a fine free way of moving it. She wore a short tunic of undyed spider silk, which exactly matched the soft curling hair that fell down her back—a bright, true silver with little peacock glints of colour in it.

Her face was one that no man would forget in a hurry. It was a face shaped warmly and generously for all the womanly things—passion and laughter and tenderness. But something had happened to it. Something had given it a bitter sulky look. There were resentment in it and deep anger and hardness—and yet, with all that, it was somehow a pathetically eager face with lost and frightened eyes.

Heath remembered vaguely a day when he would have liked to solve the riddle of that contradictory face. A day long ago, before Ethne came.

He said, speaking to both of them, "Who are you and what do you want with me?"

He looked now directly at the man and it was a look of sheer black hatred. "Didn't you have enough fun with me at Kalruna's?"

"I had to be sure of you," the stranger said. "Sure that you had not lied about the Moonfire."

He leaned forward, his eyes narrowed and piercing. He did not sit easily. His body was curved like a bent bow. In the light of the hanging lantern his scarred, handsome face showed a ripple of little muscles under the skin. A man in a hurry, Heath thought, a man with a sharp goad pricking his flanks.

"And what was that to you?" said Heath.

It was a foolish question. Already Heath knew what was coming. His whole being drew in upon itself, retreated.

The stranger did not answer directly. Instead he said. "You knew the cult that calls itself guardian of the Mysteries of the Moon."

"The oldest cult on Venus and one of the strongest. One of the strangest, too, on a moonless planet," Heath said slowly to no one in particular. "The Moonfire is their symbol of godhead."

The woman laughed without mirth. "Although," she said, "they've never seen it."

THE MOON THAT VANISHED

The stranger went on, "All Venus knows about you, David Heath. The word travels. The priests know too—the Children of the Moon. They have a special interest in you."

Heath waited. He did not speak.

"You belong to the gods for their own vengeance," the stranger said. "But the vengeance hasn't come. Perhaps because you're an Earthman and therefore less obedient to the gods of Venus. Anyway, the Children of the Moon are tired of waiting. The longer you live the more men may be tempted to blasphemy, the less faith there will be in the ability of the gods to punish men for their sins." His voice had a biting edge of sarcasm. "So," he finished, "the Children of the Moon are coming to see to it that you die."

Heath smiled. "Do the priests tell you their secrets?"

The man turned his head and said, "Alor."

The woman stepped in front of Heath and loosed her tunic at the shoulder. "There," she said furiously. "Look!"

Her anger was not with Heath. It was with what he saw. The tattoo branded between her white breasts—the round rayed symbol of the Moon.

Heath caught his breath and let it out in a long sigh. "A handmaiden of the temple," he said and looked again at her face. Her eyes met his, silvery-cold, level, daring him to say more.

"We are sold out of our cradles," she said. "We have no choice. And our families are very proud to have a daughter chosen for the temple."

Bitterness and pride and the smouldering anger of the slave.

She said, "Broca tells the truth."

*

Heath's body seemed to tighten in upon itself. He glanced from one to the other and back again, not saying anything, and his heart beat fast and hard, knocking against his ribs.

Alor said, "They will kill you and it won't be easy dying. I know. I've heard men screaming sometimes for many nights and their sin was less than yours."

Heath said out of a dry mouth, "A runaway girl from the temple gardens and a thrower of spears. Their sin is great too. They didn't come halfway across Venus just to warn me. I think they lie. I think the priests are after them."

"We're all three proscribed," said Broca, "but Alor and I could get away. You they'll hunt down no matter where you go—except one place."

12

And Heath said, "Where is that?"

"The Moonfire."

After a long while Heath uttered a harsh grating sound that might have been a laugh.

"Get out," he said. "Get away from me."

He got to his feet, shaking with weakness and fury. "You lie, both of you—because I'm the only living man who has seen the Moonfire and you want me to take you there. You believe the legends. You think the Moonfire will change you into gods. You're mad, like all the other fools, for the power and the glory you think you'll have. Well, I can tell you this—the Moonfire will give you nothing but suffering and death."

His voice rose. "Go lie to someone else. Frighten the Guardians of the Upper Seas. Bribe the gods themselves to take you there. But get away from me!"

The Venusian rose slowly. The cabin was small for him, the deck beams riding his shoulders. He swept the little dragon aside. He took Heath in his two hands and he said, "I will reach the Moonfire, and you will take me there."

Heath struck him across the face.

Sheer astonishment held Broca still for a moment and Heath said, "You're not a god yet."

The Venusian opened his mouth in a snarling grin. His hands shifted and tightened.

The woman said sharply, "Broca!" She stepped in close, wrenching at Broca's wrists. "Don't kill him, you fool!"

Broca let his breath out hard between his teeth. Gradually his hands relaxed. Heath's face was suffused with dark blood. He would have fallen if the woman had not caught him.

She said to Broca, "Strike him—but not too hard."

Broca raised his fist and struck Heath carefully on the point of the jaw.

It could not have been more than two of the long Venusian hours before Heath came to. He did that slowly as always—progressing from a vast vague wretchedness to an acute awareness of everything that was the matter with him. His head felt as though it had been cleft in two with an axe from the jaw upward.

He could not understand why he should have wakened. The drug alone should have been good for hours of heavy sleep. The sky beyond the cabin port had changed. The night was almost over. He lay for a moment, wondering whether or not he was going to be sick, and then suddenly he realized what had wakened him in spite of everything.

The *Ethne* was under way.

His anger choked him so that he could not even swear. He dragged himself to his feet and crossed the cabin, feeling even then that she was not going right, that the dawn wind was strong and she was rolling to it, yawing.

He kicked open the door and came out on deck.

The great lateen sail of golden spider silk, ghostly in the blue air, slatted and spilled wind, shaking against loose yards. Heath turned and made for the raised poop, finding strength in his fear for the ship. Broca was up there, braced against the loom of the stern sweep. The wake lay white on the black water, twisting like a snake.

The woman Alor stood at the rail, staring at the low land that lay behind them.

Broca made no protest as Heath knocked him aside and took the sweep. Alor turned and watched but did not speak.

The *Ethne* was small and the simple rig was such that one man could handle it. Heath trimmed the sail and in a few seconds she was stepping light and dainty as her namesake, her wake straight as a ruled line.

When that was done Heath turned upon them and cursed them in a fury greater than that of a woman whose child has been stolen.

Broca ignored him. He stood watching the land and the lightening sky. When Heath was all through the woman said, "We had to go. It may already be too late. And you weren't going to help."

Heath didn't say anything more. There weren't any words. He swung the helm hard over.

*

Broca was beside him in one step, his hand raised and then suddenly Alor cried out, "*Wait!*"

Something in her voice brought both men around to look at her. She stood at the rail, facing into the wind, her hair flying, the short skirt of her tunic whipped back against her thighs. Her arms were raised in a pointing gesture.

It was dawn now.

For a moment Heath lost all sense of time. The deck lifting lightly under his feet, the low mist and dawn over the Sea of Morning Opals, the dawn that gave the sea its name. It seemed that there had never been a Moonfire, never been a past or a

14

future, but only David Heath and his ship and the light coming over the water.

It came slowly, sifting down like a rain of jewels through the miles of pearl-grey cloud. Cool and slow at first, then warming and spreading, turning the misty air to drops of rosy fire, opaline, glowing, low to the water, so that the little ship seemed to be drifting through the heart of a fire-opal as vast as the universe.

The sea turned colour, from black to indigo streaked with milky bands. Flights of the small bright dragons rose flashing from the weed-beds that lay scattered on the surface in careless patterns of purple and ochre and cinnabar and the weed itself stirred with dim sentient life, lifting its tendrils to the light.

For one short moment David Heath was completely happy.

Then he saw that Broca had caught up a bow from under the taffrail. Heath realized that they must have fetched all their traps coolly aboard while he was in Kalruna's. It was one of the great longbows of the Upland barbarians and Broca bent its massive arc as though it had been a twig and laid across it a bone-barbed shaft.

A ship was coming toward them, a slender shape of pearl flying through the softly burning veils of mist. Her sail was emerald green. She was a long way off but she had the wind behind her and she was coming down with it like a swooping dragon.

"That's the *Lahal*," said Heath. "What does Johor think he's doing?"

Then he saw, with a start of incredulous horror, that on the prow of the oncoming ship the great spiked ram had been lowered into place.

During the moment when Heath's brain struggled to understand why Johor, ordinary trading skipper of an ordinary ship, should wish to sink him, Alor said five words.

"The Children of the Moon."

Now, on the *Lahal's* foredeck, Heath could distinguish four tiny figures dressed in black.

The long shining ram dipped and glittered in the dawn.

Heath flung himself against the stern sweep. The *Ethne's* golden sail cracked taut. She headed up into the wind. Heath measured his distance grimly and settled down.

Broca turned on him furiously. "Are you mad? They'll run us down! Go the other way."

Heath said, "There is no other way. They've got me pinned on a lee shore." He was suddenly full of a blind rage against Johor and the four black-clad priests.

THE MOON THAT VANISHED

There was nothing to do but wait—wait and sail the heart out of his ship and hope that enough of David Heath still lived to get them through. *And if not,* Heath thought, *I'll take the Lahal down with me!*

Broca and Alor stood by the rail together, watching the racing green sail. They did not speak. There was nothing to say. Heath saw that now and again the woman turned to study him.

The wakes of the two ships lay white on the water, two legs of a triangle rushing toward their apex.

Heath could see Johor now, manning the sweep. He could see the crew crouching in the waist, frightened sailors rounded up to do the bidding of the priests. They were armed and standing by with grapnels.

Now, on the foredeck, he could see the Children of the Moon.

They were tall men. They wore tunics of black link mail with the rayed symbol of the Moon blazed in jewels on their breasts. They rode the pitching deck, their silver hair flying loose in the wind, and their bodies were as the bodies of wolves that run down their prey and devour it.

Heath fought the stern sweep, fought the straining ship, fought with wind and distance to cheat them of their will.

And the woman Alor kept watching David Heath with her bitter challenging eyes and Heath hated her as he did the priests, with a deadly hatred, because he knew what he must took like with his beaked bony face and wasted body, swaying and shivering over the loom of the sweep.

*

Closer and closer swept the emerald sail, rounded and gleaming like a peacock's breast in the light. Pearl white and emerald, purple and gold, on a dark blue sea, the spiked ram glittering—two bright dragons racing toward marriage, toward death.

Close, very close. The rayed symbols blazed fire on the breasts of the Children of the Moon.

The woman Alor lifted her head high into the wind and cried out—a long harsh ringing cry like the scream of an eagle. It ended in a name, and she spoke it like a curse.

"*Vakor!*"

One of the priests wore the jeweled fillet that marked him leader. He flung up his arms, and the words of his malediction came hot and bitter down the wind.

Broca's bowstring thrummed like a great harp. The shaft fell short and Vakor

16

laughed.

The priests went aft to be safe from buckling timbers and the faces of the seamen were full of fear.

Heath cried out a warning. He saw Alor and Broca drop flat to the deck. He saw their faces. They were the faces of a man and a woman who were on the point of death and did not like it but were not afraid. Broca reached out and braced the woman's body with his own.

Heath shoved *Ethne's* nose fair into the wind and let her jibe.

The *Lahal* went thundering by not three yards away, helpless to do anything about it.

The kicking sweep had knocked Heath into the scuppers, half dazed. He heard the booming sail slat over, felt the wrenching shudder that shook the *Ethne* down to her last spike and prayed that the mast would stay in her. As he dragged himself back he saw that the priest Vakor had leaped onto the *Lahal's* high stern. He was close enough for Heath to see his face.

They looked into each other's eyes and the eyes of Vakor were brilliant and wild, the eyes of a fanatic. He was not old. His body was virile and strong, his face cut in fine sweeping lines, the mouth full and sensuous and proud. He was tense with cheated fury and his voice rang against the wind like the howling of a beast.

"We will follow! We will follow, and the gods will slay!"

As the rush of the *Lahal* carried him away, Heath heard the last echo of his cry.

"Alor!"

With all the strength he had left Heath quieted his outraged ship and let her fill away on the starboard tack. Broca and Alor got slowly to their feet. Broca said, "I thought you'd wrecked her."

"They had the wind of me," Heath said. "I couldn't come about like a Christian."

Alor walked to the stern and watched where the *Lahal* wallowed and staggered as she tried to stop her headlong rush. "Vakor!" she whispered, and spat into the sea.

Broca said, "They will follow us. Alor told me—they have a chart, the only one, that shows the way to the Moonfire."

Heath shrugged. He was too weary now to care. He pointed off to the right.

"There's a strong ocean current runs there, like a river in the sea. Most skippers are afraid of it but their ships aren't like the *Ethne*. We'll ride it. After that we'll have to trust to luck."

Alor swung around sharply. "Then you will go to the Moonfire."

THE MOON THAT VANISHED

"I didn't say that. Broca, get me the bottle out of my cabin locker."

But it was the woman who fetched it to him and watched him drink, then said, "Are you all right?"

"I'm dying, and she asks me that," said Heath.

She looked a moment steadily into his eyes and oddly enough there was no mockery in her voice when she spoke, only respect.

"You won't die," she said and went away.

In a few moments the current took the *Ethne* and swept her away northward. The *Lahal* vanished into the mists behind them. She was cranky in close handling and Heath knew that Johor would not dare the swirling current.

For nearly three hours he stayed at his post and took the ship through. When the ocean stream curved east he rode out of it into still water. Then he fell down on the deck and slept.

Once again the tall barbarian lifted him like a child and laid him in his bunk.

All through the rest of that day and the long Venusian night, while Broca steered, Heath lay in bitter sleep. Alor sat beside him, watching the nightmare shadows that crossed his face, listening as he moaned and talked, soothing his worst tremors.

He repeated the name of Ethne over and over again and a puzzled strangely wistful look came in the eyes of Alor.

When it was dawn again Heath awoke and went on deck. Broca said with barbarian bluntness, "Have you decided?"

Heath did not answer and Alor said, "Vakor will hunt you down. The word has gone out all over Venus, wherever there are men. There'll be no refuge for you—except one."

Heath smiled, a mirthless baring of the teeth. "And that's the Moonfire. You make it all so simple."

And yet he knew she spoke the truth. The Children of the Moon would never leave his track. He was a rat in a maze and every passage led to death.

But there were different deaths. If he had to die it would not be as Vakor willed but with Ethne—an Ethne more real than a shadow—in his arms again.

He realized now that deep in his mind he had always known, all these three seasons and more that he had clung to a life not worth the living. He had known that someday he must go back again.

"We'll go to the Moonfire," he said, "and perhaps we shall all be gods."

Broca said, "You are weak, Earthman. You didn't have the courage."

Heath said one word.

"Wait."

Over the Bar

The days and the nights went by, and the *Ethne* fled north across the Sea of Morning Opals, north toward the equator. They were far out of the trade lanes. All these vast upper reaches were wilderness. There were not even fishing villages along the coast. The great cliffs rose sheer from the water and nothing could find a foothold there. And beyond, past the Dragon's Throat, lay only the barren death-trap of the Upper Seas.

The *Ethne* ran as sweetly as though she joyed to be free again, free of the muddy harbour and the chains. And a change came over Heath. He was a man again. He stood shaved and clean and erect on his own deck and there was no decision to be made anymore, no doubt. The long dread, the long delay, were over and he too, in his own bitter way, was happy.

They had seen nothing more of the *Lahal* but Heath knew quite well that she was there somewhere, following. She was not as fleet as the *Ethne* but she was sound and Johor was a good sailor. Moreover, the priest Vakor was there and he would drive the *Lahal* over the Mountains of White Cloud if he had to—to catch them.

He said once to Alor, "Vakor seems to have a special hatred for you."

Her face twisted with revulsion and remembered shame. "He is a beast," she said. "He is a serpent, a lizard that walks like a king." She added, "We've made it easy for him, the three of us together like this."

From where he sat steering Heath looked at her with a remote curiosity. She stood, long legged, bold-mouthed, looking back with sombre smoky eyes at the white wake unrolling behind them.

He said, "You must have loved Broca to break your vows for him. Considering what it means if they catch you."

Alor looked at him, then laughed, a brief sound that had no humor in it.

"I'd have gone with any man strong enough to take me out of the temple," she said. "And Broca is strong and he worships me."

Heath was genuinely astonished. "You don't love him?"

She shrugged. "He is good to look at. He is a chief of warriors and he is a man and not a priest. But love—"

She asked suddenly, "What is it like—to love as you loved your Ethne?"

Heath started. "What do you know about Ethne?" he asked harshly.

"You have talked of her in sleep. And Broca told me how you called her shadow in Kalruna's place. You dared the Moonfire to gain her back."

She glanced at the ivory figurehead on the high curving bow, the image of a woman, young and slim and smiling.

"I think you are a fool," she said abruptly. "I think only a fool would love a shadow."

She had left him and gone down into the cabin before he could gather words, before he could take her white neck between his hands and break it.

Ethne—Ethne!

He cursed the woman of the temple gardens.

He was still in a brooding fury when Broca came up out of the cabin to relieve him at the sweep.

"I'll steer a while yet," Heath told him curtly. "I think the weather's going to break."

Clouds were boiling up in the south as the night closed down. The sea was running in long easy swells as it had done for all these days but there was a difference, a pulse and a stir that quivered all through the ship's keel.

Broca, stretching huge shoulders, looked away to the south and then down at Heath.

"I think you talk too much to my woman," he said.

Before Heath could answer the other laid his hand lightly on the Earthman's shoulder. A light grip but with strength enough behind it to crack Heath's bones.

He said, "Do not talk so much to Alor."

"I haven't sought her out," Heath snapped savagely. "She's your woman—you worry about her."

"I am not worried about her," Broca answered calmly. "Not about her and you."

He was looking down at Heath as he spoke and Heath knew the contrast they made—his own lean body and gaunt face against the big barbarian's magnificent strength.

"But she is always with you on the deck, listening to your stories of the sea," said Broca. "Do not talk to her so much," he repeated and this time there was an edge to his voice.

"For heaven's sake!" said Heath jeeringly. "If I'm a fool what are you? A man mad enough to look for power in the Moonfire and faithfulness in a temple wench! And now you're jealous."

*

He hated both Broca and Alor bitterly in this moment and out of his hate he spoke.

"Wait until the Moonfire touches you. It will break your strength and your pride. After that you won't care who your woman talks to or where."

Broca gave him a stare of unmoved contempt. Then he turned his back and settled down to look out across the darkening sea.

After a while, the amusing side of the whole thing struck Heath, and he began to laugh.

They were, all three of them, going to die. Somewhere out there to the south, Vakor came like a black shepherd, driving them toward death. Dreams of empire, dreams of glory and a voyage that tempted the vengeance of the gods—and at such a time the barbarian chief could be jealous.

With sudden shock he realized just how much time Alor had spent with him. Out of habit and custom as old as the sea he had helped to while away the long hard hours with a sailor's yarns. Looking back he could see Alor's face, strangely young and eager as she listened, could remember how she asked questions and wanted to learn the ways and the working of the ship.

He could remember now how beautiful she looked with the wind in her hair, her firm strong body holding the *Ethne* steady in a quartering sea.

The storm brewed over the hours and at last it broke.

Heath had known that the Sea of Morning Opals would not let him go without a struggle. It had tried him with shallows, with shifting reefs, with dead calms and booming solar tides and all the devices of current, fog and drifting weed. He had beaten all of them. Now he was almost within sight of the Dragon's Throat, the gateway to the Upper Seas and it was a murderous moment for a storm out of the south.

The night had turned black. The sea burned with white phosphorescence, a boiling cauldron of witch-fire. The wind was frightening. The *Ethne* plunged and staggered, driving under a bare pole, and for once Heath was glad of Broca's strength as they fought the sweep together.

He became aware that someone was beside him and knew that it was Alor.

"Go below!" he yelled and caught only the echo of her answer. She did not go but

21

threw her weight too against the sweep.

Lightning-bolts as broad as comet's tails came streaking down with a rush and a fury as though they had started their run from another star and gathered speed across half the galaxy. They lit the Sea of Morning Opals with a purple glare until the thunder brought the darkness crashing down again. Then the rain fell like a river rolling down the belts of cloud.

Heath groaned inwardly. The wind and the following sea had taken the little ship between them and were hurling her forward. At the speed she was making now she would hit the Dragon's Throat at dawn. She would hit it full tilt and helpless as a drifting chip.

The lightning showed him the barbarian's great straining body, gleaming wet, his long hair torn loose from its knots and chains, streaming with wind and water. It showed him Alor too. Their hands and their shoulders touched, straining together.

It seemed that they struggled on that way for centuries and then, abruptly, the rain stopped, the wind slackened, and there was a period of eerie silence. Alor's voice sounded loud in Heath's ears, crying, "Is it over?"

"No," he answered. "Listen!"

They heard a deep and steady booming, distant in the north—the boom of surf. The storm began again.

Dawn came, hardly lighter than the night. Through the flying wrack Heath could see cliffs on either side where the mountain ranges narrowed in, funneling the Sea of Morning Opals into the strait of the Dragon's Throat. The driven sea ran high between them, bursting white against the black rock.

The *Ethne* was carried headlong, a leaf in a millrace.

The cliffs drew in and in until there was a gap of no more than a mile between them. Black brooding titans and the space below a fury of white water, torn and shredded by fang-like rocks.

The Dragon's Throat.

When he had made the passage before Heath had had fair weather and men for the oars. Even then it had not been easy. Now he tried to remember where the channel lay, tried to force the ship toward what seemed to be an open lane among the rocks.

The *Ethne* gathered speed and shot forward into the Dragon's Throat.

She fled through a blind insanity of spray and wind and sound. Time and again Heath saw the loom of a towering rock before him and wrenched the ship aside or fought to keep away from death that was hidden just under the boiling surface. Twice, three times, the *Ethne* gave a grating shudder and he thought she was gone.

Once, toward the last, when it seemed that there was no hope, he felt Alor's hand close over his.

The high water saved them, catching them in its own rush down the channel, carrying them over the rocks and finally over the bar at the end of the gut. The *Ethne* came staggering out into the relative quiet of the Upper Seas, where the pounding waves seemed gentle and it was all done so quickly, over so soon. For a long time the three of them stood sagging over the sweep, not able to realize that it was over and they still lived.

The storm spent itself. The wind settled to a steady blow. Heath got a rag of sail up. Then he sat down by the tiller and bowed his head over his knees and thought about how Alor had caught his hand when she believed she was going to die.

"I WILL WAIT!"

Even this early it was hot. The Upper Seas sprawled along the equator, shallow landlocked waters choked with weed and fouled with shifting reefs of mud, cut into a maze of lakes and blind channels by the jutting headlands of the mountains.

The wind dropped to a flat calm. They left the open water behind them, where it was swept clean by the tides from the Sea of Morning Opals. The floating weed thickened around them, a blotched ochre plain that stirred with its own dim mindless life. The air smelled rotten.

Under Heath's direction they swung the weed-knife into place, the great braced blade that fitted over the prow. Then, using the heavy sweep as a sculling oar, they began to push the *Ethne* forward by the strength of their sweating backs.

Clouds of the little bright-scaled dragons rose with hissing screams, disturbed by the ship. This was their breeding ground. They fought and nested in the weed and the steaming air was full of the sound of their wings. They perched on the rail and in the rigging, watching with their red eyes. The creature that rode Heath's shoulder emitted harsh cries of excitement. Heath tossed him into the air and he flew away to join his mates.

There was life under the weed, spawning in the hot stagnant waters, multiform and formless, swarming, endlessly hungry. Small reptilian creatures flopped and slithered through the weed, eating the dragon's eggs, and here and there a flat dark head would break through with a snap and a crunch, and it would watch the *Ethne* with incurious eyes while it chewed and swallowed.

Constantly Heath kept watch.

The sun rose high above the eternal clouds. The heat seeped down and gathered. The scull moved back and forth, the knife bit, the weed dragged against the hull and behind them the cut closed slowly as the stuff wrapped and coiled upon itself.

Heath's eyes kept turning to Alor.

He did not want to look at her. He did not wish to remember the touch of her hand on his. He wished only to remember Ethne, to remember the agony of the Moonfire and to think of the reward that lay beyond it if he could endure. What could a temple wench mean to him beside that?

But he kept looking at her covertly. Her white limbs glistened with sweat and her red mouth was sullen with weariness and even so there was a strange wild beauty about her. Time and again her gaze would meet his, a quick hungry glance from under her lashes, and her eyes were not the eyes of a temple wench. Heath cursed Broca in his heart for making him think of Alor and he cursed himself because now he could not stop thinking of her.

They toiled until they could not stand. Then they sprawled on the deck in the breathless heat to rest. Broca pulled Alor to him.

"Soon this will all be over," he said. "Soon we will reach the Moonfire. You will like that, Alor—to be mated to a god!"

She lay unresponsive in the circle of his arm, her head turned away. She did not answer.

Broca laughed. "God and goddess. Two of a kind as we are now. We'll build our thrones so high the sun can see them." He rolled her head on his shoulder, looking down intently into her face. "Power, Alor. Strength. We will have them together." He covered her mouth with his, and his free hand caressed her, deliberate, possessive.

She thrust him away. "Don't," she said angrily. "It's too hot and I'm too tired." She got up and walked to the side, standing with her back to Broca.

Broca looked at her. Then he turned and looked at Heath. A dark flush reddened his skin. He said slowly, "Too hot and too tired—and besides, the Earthman is watching."

He sprang up and caught Alor and swung her around, one huge hand tangled in her hair, holding her. As soon as he touched her Heath also sprang up and said harshly, "Let her alone!"

Broca said, "She is my mate but I may not touch her." He glared down into Alor's blazing eyes and said, "She is my mate—or isn't she?"

He flung her away. He turned his head from side to side, half blind with rage.

"Do you think I didn't see you?" he asked thickly. "All day, looking at each other."

Heath said, "You're crazy."

"Yes," answered Broca, "I am." He took two steps toward Heath and added, "Crazy enough to kill you."

Alor said, "If you do you'll never reach the Moonfire."

Broca paused, trapped for one moment between his passion and his dream. He was facing the stern. Something caused his gaze to waver from Heath and then, gradually, his expression changed. Heath swung around and Alor gave a smothered cry.

Far behind them, vague in the steaming air, was an emerald sail.

*

The *Lahal* must have come through the Dragon's Throat as soon as the storm was over. With men to man the rowing benches she had gained on the *Ethne* during the calm. Now she too was in the weed, and the oars were useless but there were men to scull her. She would move faster than the *Ethne* and without pause.

There would be little rest for Heath and Broca and the woman.

They swayed at the sculling oar all the stifling afternoon and all the breathless night, falling into the dull, half-hypnotized rhythm of beasts who walk forever around a water-wheel. Two of them working always, while the third slept, and Broca never took his eyes from Alor. With his tremendous vitality it seemed that he never slept and during the periods when Heath and Alor were alone at the oar together they exchanged neither words nor glances.

At dawn they saw that the *Lahal* was closer.

Broca crouched on the deck. He lifted his head and looked at the green sail. Heath saw that his eyes were very bright and that he shivered in spite of the brooding heat.

Heath's heart sank. The Upper Seas were rank with fever, and it looked as though the big barbarian was in for a bad go of it. Heath himself was pretty well immune to it but Broca was used to the clean air of the High Plateaus and the poison was working in his blood.

He measured the speed of the two ships and said, "It's no use. We must stand

and fight."

Heath said savagely, "I thought you wanted to find the Moonfire. I thought you were the strong man who could win through it where everybody else has failed. I thought you were going to be a god."

Broca got to his feet. "With fever or without it I'm a better man than you."

"Then work! If we can just keep ahead of them until we clear the weed—"

Broca said, "The Moonfire?"

"Yes."

"We will keep ahead."

He bent his back to the scull and the *Ethne* crept forward through the weed. Her golden sail hung from the yard with a terrible stillness. The heat pressed down upon the Upper Seas as though the sun itself were falling through the haze. Astern the *Lahal* moved steadily on.

Broca's fever mounted. He turned from time to time to curse Vakor, shouting at the emerald sail.

"You'll never catch us, priest!" he would cry. "I am Broca of the tribe of Sarn and I will beat you—and I will beat the Moonfire. You will lie on your belly, priest, and lick my sandals before you die."

Then he would turn to Alor, his eyes shining. "You know the legends, Alor! The man who can bathe in the heart of the Moonfire has the power of the High Ones. He can build a world to suit himself, he can be king and lord and master. He can give his woman-god a palace of diamonds with a floor of gold. That is true, Alor. You have heard the priests say it in the temple."

Alor answered, "It is true."

"A new world, Alor. A world of our own."

He made the great sweep swing in a frenzy of strength and once again the mystery of the Moonfire swept over Heath. Why, since the priests knew the way there, did they not themselves become gods. Why had no man ever come out of it with godhead—only a few, a handful like himself, who had not had the valor to go all the way in.

*

And yet there was godhead there. He knew because within himself there was the shadow of it.

The endless day wore on. The emerald sail came closer.

Toward mid-afternoon there was a sudden clattering flight of the little dragons

26

and all life stopped still in the weed. The reptilian creatures lay motionless with dragon's eggs unbroken in their jaws. No head broke the surface to feed. The dragons flew away in a hissing cloud. There was utter silence.

Heath flung himself against the sweep and stopped it.

"Be quiet," he said. "Look. Out there."

They followed his gesture. Far away over the port bow, flowing toward them, was a ripple in the weed. A ripple as though the very bed of the Upper Seas was in motion.

"What is it?" whispered Alor, and saw Heath's face, and was silent.

Sluggishly, yet with frightened speed, the ripple came toward them. Heath got a harpoon out of the stern locker. He watched the motion of the weed, saw it gradually slow and stop in a puzzled way. Then he threw the harpoon as far away from the ship as he could with all his strength and more.

The ripple began again. It swerved and sped toward where the harpoon had fallen.

"They'll attack anything that moves," said Heath. "It lost us because we stopped. Watch."

The weed heaved and burst open, its meshes snapping across a scaled and titanic back. There seemed to be no shape to the creature, no distinguishable head. It was simply a vast and hungry blackness that spread upward and outward and the luckless brutes that cowered near it hissed and thrashed in their efforts to escape, and were engulfed and vanished.

Again Alor whispered, "What is it?"

"One of the Guardians," Heath answered. "The Guardians of the Upper Seas. They will crush a moving ship to splinters and eat the crew."

He glanced back at the *Lahal*. She, too, had come to a dead stop. The canny Vakor had scented the danger also.

"We'll have to wait," said Heath, "until it goes away."

They waited. The huge shape of darkness sucked and floundered in the weed and was in no hurry to go.

Broca sat staring at Heath. He was deep in fever and his eyes were not sane. He began to mutter to himself, incoherent ramblings in which only the name Alor and the word Moonfire were distinguishable.

Suddenly, with startling clarity, he said, "The Moonfire is nothing without Alor."

He repeated "Nothing!" several times, beating his huge fists on his knees each time he said it. Then he turned his head blindly from side to side as though looking for something. "She's gone. Alor's gone. She's gone to the Earthman."

Alor spoke to him, touched him, but he shook her off. In his fever-mad brain there was only one truth. He rose and went toward David Heath.

Heath got up. "Broca!" he said. "Alor is there beside you. She hasn't gone!"

Broca did not hear. He did not stop.

Alor cried out, "*Broca!*"

"No," said Broca. "You love him. You're not mine anymore. When you look at me I am nothing. Your lips have no warmth in them." He reached out toward David Heath and he was blind and deaf to everything but the life that was in him to be torn out and trampled upon and destroyed.

In the cramped space of the afterdeck there was not much room to move. Heath did not want to fight. He tried to dodge the sick giant but Broca pinned him against the rail. Fever or no fever, Heath had to fight him and it was not much use. Broca was beyond feeling pain.

His sheer weight crushed Heath against the rail, bent his spine almost to breaking and his hands found Heath's throat. Heath struck and struck again and wondered if he had come all this way to die in a senseless quarrel over a woman.

Abruptly he realized that Broca was letting go, was sliding down against him to the deck. Through a swimming haze he saw Alor standing there with a belaying pin in her hand. He began to tremble, partly with reaction but mostly with fury that he should have needed a woman's help to save his life. Broca lay still, breathing heavily.

"Thanks," said Heath curtly. "Too bad you had to hit him. He didn't know what he was doing."

Alor said levelly, "Didn't he?"

*

Heath did not answer. He started to turn away and she caught him, forcing him to look at her.

"Very likely I will die in the Moonfire," she said. "I haven't the faith in my strength that Broca has. So I'm going to say this now—I love you, David Heath. I don't care what you think or what you do about it but I love you."

Her eyes searched his face, as though she wanted to remember every line and plane of it. Then she kissed him and her mouth was tender and very sweet.

She stepped back and said quietly, "I think the Guardian has gone. The *Lahal* is under way again."

Heath followed her without a word to the sweep. Her kiss burned in him like sweet fire. He was shaken and utterly confused.

They toiled together while Broca slept. They dared not pause. Heath could distinguish the men now aboard the *Lahal*, little bent figures sculling, sculling, and there were always fresh ones. He could see the black tunics of the Children of the Moon who stood upon the foredeck and waited.

The *Ethne* moved more and more slowly as the hours passed and the gap between the two ships grew steadily smaller. Night came and through the darkness they could hear the voice of Vakor howling after them.

Toward midnight Broca roused. The fever had left him but he was morose and silent. He thrust Alor roughly aside and took the sweep and the *Ethne* gathered speed.

"How much farther?" he asked. And Heath panted, "Not far now."

Dawn came and still they were not clear of the weed. The *Lahal* was so near them now that Heath could see the jeweled fillet on Vakor's brow. He stood alone, high on the upper brace of the weed-knife, and he watched them, laughing.

"Work!" he shouted at them. "Toil and sweat! You, Alor—woman of the gardens! This is better than the Temple. Broca—thief and breaker of the Law—strain your muscles there! And you, Earthman. For the second time you defy the gods!" He leaned out over the weed as though he would reach ahead and grasp the *Ethne* in his bare hands and drag her back.

"Sweat and strain, you dogs! You can't escape!"

And they did sweat and strain and fresh relays of men worked at the sweep of the *Lahal*, breaking their hearts to go faster and ever faster. Vakor laughed from his high perch and it seemed futile for the *Ethne* to go on any longer with this lost race.

But Heath looked ahead with burning sunken eyes. He saw how the mists rose and gathered to the north, how the color of the weed changed, and he urged the others on. There was a fury in him now. It blazed brighter and harder than Broca's, this iron fury that would not, by the gods themselves, be balked of the Moonfire.

They kept ahead—so little ahead that the *Lahal* was almost within arrow-shot of them. Then the weed thinned and the *Ethne* began to gain a little and suddenly, before they realized it, they were in open water.

Like mad creatures they worked the scull and Heath steered the *Ethne* where he remembered the northern current ran, drawn by The-Ocean-That-Is-Not-Water.

After the terrible labour of the weed it seemed that they were flying. But as the mists began to wreath about them the *Lahal* too had freed herself and was racing toward them with every man on the rowing benches.

The mists thickened around them. The black water began to have a rare occasional hint of gold, like shooting sparks beneath the surface. There began to be islands, low and small, rank with queer vegetation. The flying dragons did not come here nor the Guardians nor the little reptiles. It was very hot and very still.

Through the stillness the voice of Vakor rose in a harsh wild screaming as he cursed the rowers on.

The current grew more swift and the dancing flecks of gold brightened in the water. Heath's face bore a strange unhuman look. The oars of the *Lahal* beat and churned and bowmen stood now on the foredeck, ready to shoot when they came within range.

Then, incredibly, Vakor gave one long high scream and flung up his hand and the oars stopped. Vakor stretched both arms above his head, his fists clenched, and he hurled after them one terrible word of malediction.

"I will wait, blasphemers! If so be you live I will be here—waiting!"

The emerald sail dwindled in the *Ethne's* wake, faded and was lost in the mist.

Broca said, "They had us. Why did they stop?"

Heath pointed. Up ahead the whole misty north was touched with a breath of burning gold.

"The Moonfire!"

Into the Moonfire

This was the dream that had driven Heath to madness, the nightmare that had haunted him, the memory that had drawn him back in spite of terror and the certainty of destruction. Now it was reality and he could not separate it from the dream.

Once again he watched the sea change until the *Ethne* drifted not on water but on a golden liquid that lapped her hull with soft rippling fire. Once again the mist enwrapped him, shining, glowing.

The first faint tingling thrill moved in his blood and he knew how it would be—the lying pleasure that mounted through ecstasy to unendurable pain. He saw the dim islands, low and black, a maze through which a ship might wander forever without finding the source that poured out this wonder of living light.

He saw the bones of ships that had died searching. They lay on the island beaches and the mist made them a bright shroud. There were not many of them. Some were so old that the race that built them had vanished out of the memory of Venus.

The hushed unearthly beauty wrenched Heath's heart and he was afraid unto dying and yet filled with lust, with a terrible hunger.

Broca drew the air deep into his lungs as though he would suck the power out of the Moonfire.

"Can you find it again?" he asked. "The heart of it."

"I can find it."

Alor stood silent and unmoving. She was all silver in this light, dusted with golden motes.

Heath said, "Are you afraid, breaking the tabu?"

"Habit is hard to break." She turned to him and asked, "What is the Moonfire?"

"Haven't the priests told you?"

"They say that Venus once had a moon. It rode in the clouds like a disc of fire and the god who dwelt within it was supreme over all the other gods. He watched the surface of the planet and all that was done upon it. But the lesser gods were jealous, and one day they were able to destroy the palace of the Moon-god.

"All the sky of Venus was lighted by that destruction. Mountains fell and seas poured out of their beds and whole nations died. The Moon-god was slain and his shining body fell like a meteor through the clouds.

"But a god cannot really die. He only sleeps and waits. The golden mist is the cloud of his breathing, and the shining of his body is the Moonfire. A man may gain divinity from the heart of the sleeping god but all the gods of Venus will curse him if he tries because man has no right to steal their powers."

"And you don't believe that story," said Heath.

Alor shrugged. "You have seen the Moonfire. The priests have not."

"I didn't get to the heart of it," Heath said. "I only saw the edge of the crater and the light that comes up out of it, the lovely hellish light."

He stopped, shuddering, and brooded as he had so many times before on the truth behind the mystery of the Moonfire. Presently he said slowly, "There was a moon, of course, or there could be no conception of one in folklore. I believe it was radioactive, some element that hasn't been found yet or doesn't exist at all on Earth or Mars."

"I don't understand," said Alor. "What is 'radioactive'?" She used the Terran word, as Heath had, because there was no term for it in Venusian.

"It's a strange sort of fire that burns in certain elements. It eats them away, feeding on its own atoms, and the radiation from this fire is very powerful." He was silent for a moment, his eyes half closed. "Can't you feel it?" he asked. "The first little fire that burns in your own blood?"

"Yes," Alor whispered. "I feel it."

And Broca said, "It is like wine."

Heath went on, putting the old, old thoughts into words. "The moon was destroyed. Not by jealous gods but by collision with another body, perhaps an asteroid. Or maybe it was burst apart by its own blazing energy. I think that a fragment of it survived and fell here and that its radiation permeated and changed the sea and the air around it.

"It changes men in the same way. It seems to alter the whole electrical set-up of the brain, to amplify its power far beyond anything human. It gives the mind a force of will strong enough to control the free electrons in the air—to create...."

He paused, then finished quietly, "In my case, only shadows. And when that mutation occurs a man doesn't need the gods of Venus to curse him. I got only a little of it but that was enough."

*

Broca said, "It is worth bearing pain to become a god. You had no strength."

Heath smiled crookedly. "How many gods have come out of the Moonfire?"

Broca answered, "There will be one soon." Then he caught Alor by the shoulders and pulled her to him, looking down into her face. "No," he said. "Not one. Two."

"Perhaps," said Heath, "there will be three."

Broca turned and gave him a chill and level look. "I do not think," he said, "that your strength is any greater now."

After that, for a long while, they did not speak. The *Ethne* drifted on, gliding on the slow currents that moved between the islands. Sometimes they sculled, the great blade of the sweep hidden in a froth of flame. The golden glow brightened and grew and with it grew the singing fire in their blood.

Heath stood erect and strong at the helm, the old Heath who had sailed the Straits of Lhiva in the teeth of a summer gale and laughed about it. All weariness, all pain, all weakness, were swept away. It was the same with the others. Alor's head was high and Broca leaped up beside the figurehead and gave a great ringing shout.

a challenge to all the gods there were to stop him.

Heath found himself looking into Alor's eyes. She smiled, an aching thing of tears and tenderness and farewell.

"I think none of us will live," she whispered. "May you find your shadow, David, before you die."

Then Broca had turned toward them once more and the moment was gone.

Within the veil of the Moonfire there was no day nor night nor time. Heath had no idea how long the *Ethne's* purple hull rode the golden current. The tingling force spread through his whole body and pulsed and strengthened until he was drunk with the pleasure of it and the islands slipped by, and there was no sound or movement but their own in all that solemn sea.

And at last he saw ahead of him the supernal brightness that poured from the heart of the Moonfire, the living core of all the brightness of the mist. He saw the land, lifting dark and vague, drowned in the burning haze, and he steered toward it along the remembered way. There was no fear in him now. He was beyond fear.

Broca cried out suddenly, "A ship!"

Heath nodded. "It was there before. It will be there when the next man finds his way here."

Two long arms of the island reached out to form a ragged bay. The *Ethne* entered it. They passed the derelict, floating patiently, untouched here by wind or tide or ocean rot. Her blue sail was furled, her rigging all neat and ready. She waited to begin the voyage home. She would wait a long, long time.

As they neared the land they sighted other ships. They had not moved nor changed since Heath had seen them last, three years ago.

A scant few they were, that had lived to find the Dragon's Throat and pass it, that had survived the Upper Seas and the island maze of the Moonfire and had found their goal at last. Some of them floated still where their crews had left them, their sad sails drooping from the yards.

Others lay on their sides on the beach, as though in sleep. There were strange old keels that had not been seen on the seas of Venus for a thousand years. The golden mist preserved them and they waited like a pack of faithful dogs for their masters to return.

Heath brought the *Ethne* into shore at the same spot where he had beached her before. She grounded gently and he led the way over the side. He remembered the queer crumbling texture of the dark earth under his feet. He was shaken with the force that throbbed in his flesh. As before it hovered now on the edge of pain.

He led the way inland and no one spoke.

The mist thickened around them, filled with dancing sparks of light. The bay was lost behind its wreathing curtain. They walked forward and the ground began to rise under their feet slowly. They moved as in a dream and the light and the silence crushed them with a great awe.

They came upon a dead man.

He lay upon his face, his arms stretched out toward the mystery that lay beyond, his hands still yearning toward the glory he had never reached. They did not disturb him.

Mist, heavier, the glow brightening, the golden motes whirling and flickering in a madder dance. Heath listened to the voice of pain that spoke within him, rising with every step he took toward a soundless scream.

I remember, I remember! The bones, the flesh, the brain, each atom of them a separate flame, bursting, tearing to be free. I cannot go on, I cannot bear it! Soon I shall waken, safe in the mud behind Kalruna's.

But he did not wake and the ground rose steadily under his feet and there was a madness on him, a passion and a suffering that were beyond man's strength to endure. Yet he endured.

The swirling motes began to shape themselves into vague figures, formless giants that towered and strode around them. Heath heard Alor's moan of terror and forced himself to say, "They're nothing. Shadows out of our own minds. The beginning of the power."

Farther they went and farther still, and then at last Heath stopped and flung up his arm to point, looking at Broca.

"Your godhead lies there. Go and take it!"

The eyes of the barbarian were dazed and wild, fixed on the dark dim line of the crater that showed in the distance, fixed on the incredible glory that shone there.

"It beats," he whispered, "like the beating of a heart."

Alor drew back, away from him, staring at the light. "I am afraid," she said. "I will not go." Heath saw that her face was agonized, her body shaken like his own. Her voice rose in a wail. "I can't go! I can't stand it. I'm dying!" Suddenly she caught Heath's hands. "David, take me back. *Take me back!*"

Before he could think or speak Broca had torn Alor away from him and struck him a great swinging blow. Heath fell to the ground and the last thing he heard was

Alor's voice crying his name.

END OF THE DREAM

Heath was not unconscious long, for when he lifted his head again he could still see the others in the distance. Broca was running like a madman up the slope of the crater, carrying Alor in his arms. Ghostly and indistinct, he stood for an instant on the edge. Then he leaped over and was gone.

Heath was alone.

He lay still, fighting to keep his mind steady, struggling against the torture of his flesh.

"Ethne, Ethne," he whispered. "This is the end of the dream."

He began to crawl, inch by bitter inch, toward the heart of the Moonfire.

He was closer to it now than he had been before. The strange rough earth cut his hands and his bare knees. The blood ran but the pain of it was less than a pinprick against the cosmic agony of the Moonfire. Broca must have suffered too, yet he had gone running to his fate. Perhaps his nervous system was duller, more resistant to shock. Or perhaps it was simply that his lust for power carried him on.

Heath had no wish for power. He did not wish to be a god. He wished only to die and he knew that he was going to very soon. But before he died he would do what he had failed to do before. He would bring Ethne back. He would hear her voice again and look into her eyes and they would wait together for the final dark.

Her image would vanish with his death, for then mind and memory would be gone. But he would not see the life go out of her as he had all those years ago by the Sea of Morning Opals. She would be with him until the end, sweet and loving and merry, as she had always been.

He said her name over and over again as he crawled. He tried to think of nothing else, so that he might forget the terrible unhuman things that were happening within him.

"Ethne, Ethne," he whispered. His hands clawed the earth and his knees scraped it and the brilliance of the Moonfire wrapped him in golden banners of mist. Yet he would not stop, though the soul was shaken out of him.

He reached the edge of the crater and looked down upon the heart of the Moonfire.

The whole vast crater was a sea of glowing vapor, so dense that it moved in little rippling waves, tipped with a sparkling froth. There was an island in that sea, a shape like a fallen mountain that burned with a blinding intensity, so great that only the eyes of a god could bear to look at it.

It rode in the clouds like a disc of fire.

Heath knew that his guess was right. It did not matter. Body of a sleeping god or scrap of a fallen moon—it would bring Ethne back to him and for that was all he cared.

He dragged himself over the edge and let himself go, down the farther slope. He screamed once when the vapor closed over him.

After that there was a period of utter strangeness.

It seemed that some force separated the atoms that composed the organism called David Heath and reshuffled them into a different pattern. There was a wrench, an agony beyond anything he had known before and then, abruptly, the pain was gone. His body felt well and whole, his mind was awake, alert and clear with a dawning awareness of new power.

He looked down at himself, ran his hands over his face. He had not changed. And yet he knew that he was different. He had taken the full force of the radiation this time and apparently it had completed the change begun three years ago. He was not the same David Heath, perhaps, but he was no longer trapped in the no-man's-land between the old and the new.

He no longer felt that he was going to die and he no longer wished to. He was filled with a great strength and a great joy. He could bring his Ethne back now and they could live on together here in the golden garden of the Moonfire.

It would have to be here. He was sure of that. He had only been into the fringe of the Moonfire before, but he did not believe that that was the whole reason why he could create nothing but shadows. There was not a sufficient concentration of the raw energy upon which the mind's telekinetic power worked.

Probably, even in the outer mists of the Moonfire, there were not enough free electrons. But here, close to the source, the air was raging with them. Raw stuff of matter, to be shaped and formed.

David Heath rose to his feet. He lifted his head and his arms reached out longingly. Straight and shining and strong he stood in the living light and his dark face was the face of a happy god.

"Ethne," he whispered. "Ethne." This is not the end of the dream, but the beginning!

And she came.

By the power, the exultant strength that was in him, Heath brought her out of the Moonfire. Ethne, slim and smiling, indistinct at first, a shadow in the mist, but growing clearer, coming toward him. He could see her white limbs, the pale flame of her hair, her red mouth bold and sweet, her wistful eyes.

Heath recoiled with a cry. It was not Ethne who stood before him. It was Alor.

For a time he could not move but stared at what he had created. The apparition smiled at him and her face was the face of a woman who has found love and with it the whole world.

"No," he said. "It isn't you I want. It's Ethne!" He struck the thought of Alor from his mind and the image faded and once again he called Ethne to him.

*

And when she came it was not Ethne but Alor.

He destroyed the vision. Rage and disappointment almost too great to bear drove him to wander in the fog. Alor, Alor! Why did that wench of the temple gardens haunt him now?

He hated her, yet her name sang in his heart and would not be silenced. He could not forget how she had kissed him and how her eyes had looked then and how her last desperate cry had been for him.

He could not forget that his own heart had shaped her image while only his mind, his conscious mind, had said the name of Ethne.

He sat down and bent his head over his knees and wept, because he knew now that this was the end of the dream. He had lost the old love forever without knowing it. It was a cruel thing, but it was true. He had to make his peace with it.

And already Alor might be dead.

That thought cut short his grieving for what was gone. He leaped up, filled with dread. He stood for a moment, looking wildly about, and the vapor was like golden water so that he could see only a few feet away. Then he began to run, shouting her name.

For what might have been centuries in that timeless place he ran, searching for her. There was no answer to his cries. Sometimes he would see a dim figure crouching in the mist, and he would think that he had found her but each time it was the body of a man, dead for God knew how long. They were all alike. They were emaciated, as though they had died of starvation and they were all smiling. There seemed to be lost visions still in their open eyes.

THE MOON THAT VANISHED

These were the gods of the Moonfire—the handful of men through all the ages who had fought their way through to the ultimate goal.

Heath saw the cruelty of the jest. A man could find godhead in the golden lake. He could create his own world within it. But he could never leave it unless he were willing to leave also the world in which he was king. They would have learned that, these men, as they started back toward the harbor, away from the source.

Or perhaps there was more to it. Perhaps they never tried to leave.

Heath went on through the beautiful unchanging mist, calling Alor's name, and there was no answer. He realized that it was becoming more difficult for him to keep his mind on his quest. Half-formed images flickered vaguely around him. He grew excited and there was an urgency in him to stop and bring the visions clear, to build and create.

He fought off the temptation but there came a time when he had to stop because he was too tired to go on. He sank down and the hopelessness of his search came over him. Alor was gone and he could never find her. In utter dejection he crouched there, his face buried in his hands, thinking of her, and all at once he heard her voice speaking his name. He started up and she was there, holding out her hands to him.

He caught her to him and stroked her hair and kissed her, half sobbing with joy at having found her. Then a sudden thought came to him. He drew back and said, "Are you really Alor or only the shadow of my mind?"

She did not answer but only held up her mouth to be kissed again.

Heath turned away, too weary and hopeless even to destroy the vision. And then he thought, "Why should I destroy it? If the woman is lost to me why shouldn't I keep the dream?"

He looked at her again and she was Alor, clothed in warm flesh, eager-eyed.

The temptation swept over him again and this time he did not fight it. He was a god, whether he wished it or not. He would create.

He threw the whole force of his mind against the golden mist, and the intoxication of sheer power made him drunk and mad with joy.

The glowing cloud drew back to become a horizon and a sky. Under Heath's feet an island grew, warm sweet earth, rich with grass and rioting with flowers, a paradise lost in a dreaming sea. Wavelets whispered on the wide beaches, the drooping fronds of the liha-trees stirred lazily in the wind and bright birds darted, singing. Snug in the little cove a ship floated, a lovely thing that angels might have built.

Perfection, the unattainable wish of the soul. And Alor was with him to share it.

He knew now why no one had ever come out of the Moonfire.

He took the vision of Alor by the hand. He wandered with it along the beaches and presently he was aware of something missing. He smiled, and once again the little dragon rode his shoulder and he stroked it and there was no least flaw in this Elysium. David Heath had found his godhead.

But some stubborn corner of his heart betrayed him. It said, *This is all a lie and Alor waits for you. If you tarry you and she will be as those others, who are dead and smiling in the Moonfire.*

He did not want to listen. He was happy. But something made him listen and he knew that as long as the real Alor lived he could not really be content with a dream. He knew that he must destroy this paradise before it destroyed him. He knew that the Moonfire was a deadly thing and that men could not be given the power of gods and continue sane.

And yet he could not destroy the island. He could not!

Horror overcame him that he had so far succumbed, that he could no longer control his own will. And he destroyed the island and the sea and the lovely ship and it was harder than if he had torn his own flesh from the bones.

And he destroyed the vision of Alor.

He knew that if he wished to escape the madness and the death of the Moonfire he must not again create so much as a blade of grass. Nothing. Because he would never again have the strength to resist the unholy joy of creation.

TO WALK DIVINE

Once more he ran shouting through the golden fog. And it might have been a year or only a moment later that he heard Alor's voice very faintly in the distance, calling his name.

He followed the sound, crying out more loudly, but he did not hear her again. Then, looming in shadowy grandeur through the mist, he saw a castle. It was a typical Upland stronghold but it was larger than the castle of any barbarian king and it was built out of one huge crimson jewel of the sort called Dragon's Blood.

Heath knew that he was seeing part of Broca's dream.

Steps of beaten gold led up to a greater door. Two tall warriors, harness blazing with gems, stood guard. Heath went between them and they caught and held him fast. Broca's hatred for the Earthman was implicit in the beings his mind created.

Heath tried to tear himself free but their strength was more than human. They took him down fantastic corridors, over floors of pearl and crystal and precious metals. The walls were lined with open chests, full of every sort of treasure the barbarian mind could conceive. Slaves went silent-footed on their errands and the air was heavy with perfume and spices. Heath thought how strange it was to walk through the halls of another man's dream.

He was brought into a vast room where many people feasted. There were harpists and singers and dancing girls and throngs of slaves, men who wrestled and men who fought and danced with swords. The men and women at the long tables looked like chieftains and their wives but they wore plain leather and tunics without decoration, so that Broca's guardsmen and even his slaves were more resplendent than they.

Above the shouting and the revelry Broca sat, high on a throne-chair that was made like a silver dragon with its jeweled wings spread wide. He wore magnificent harness and a carved diamond that only a high king may wear hung between his eyebrows. He drank wine out of a golden cup and watched the feasting with eyes that had in them no smallest flicker of humanity. God or demon, Broca was no longer a man.

Alor sat beside him. She wore the robes of a queen but her face was hidden in her hands and her body was still as death.

Heath's cry carried across all the noise of the feast. Broca leaped to his feet and an abrupt silence fell. Everyone, guards, chieftains and slaves, turned to watch as Heath was led toward the throne—and they all hated him as Broca hated.

Alor raised her head and looked into his eyes. And she asked, in his own words, "Are you really David or only the shadow of my mind?"

"I am David," he told her and was glad he had destroyed his paradise.

Broca's mad gaze fixed on Heath. "I didn't think you had the strength," he said, and then he laughed. "But you're not a god! You stand there captive and you have no power."

Heath knew that he could fight Broca on his own grounds but he did not dare. One taste of that ecstasy had almost destroyed him. If he tried it again he knew that he and the barbarian would hurl their shadow-armies against each other as long as they lived and he would be as mad as Broca.

He looked about him at the hostile creatures who were solid and real enough to kill him at Broca's word. Then he said to Alor, "Do you wish to stay here now?"

"I wish to go out of the Moonfire with you, David, if I can. If not I wish to die."

The poison had not touched her yet. She had come without desire. Though she had bathed in the Moonfire she was still sane.

Heath turned to Broca. "You see, she isn't worthy of you."

Broca's face was dark with fury. He took Alor between his great hands and said, "You will stay with me. You're part of me. Listen, Alor. There's nothing I can't give you. I'll build other castles, other tribes, and I'll subdue them and put them in your lap. God and goddess together, Alor! We'll reign in glory."

"I'm no goddess," Alor said. "Let me go."

And Broca said, "I'll kill you, first." His gaze lowered on Heath. "I'll kill you both."

Heath said, "Do the high gods stoop to tread on ants and worms? We don't deserve such honor, she and I. We're weak and even the Moonfire can't give us strength."

He saw the flicker of thought in Broca's face and went on. "You're all-powerful, there's nothing you can't do. Why burden yourself with a mate too weak to worship you? Create another Alor, Broca! Create a goddess worthy of you!"

After a moment Alor said, "Create a woman who can love you, Broca, and let us go."

For a time there was silence in the place. The feasters and the dancers and the slaves stood without moving and their eyes glittered in the eerie light. And then Broca nodded.

"It is well," he said. "Stand up, Alor."

*

She stood. The look of power came into the face of the tall barbarian, the wild joy of molding heart's desire out of nothingness. Out of the golden air he shaped another Alor. She was not a woman but a thing of snow and flame and wonder, so that beside her the reality appeared drab and beautiless. She mounted the throne and sat beside her creator and put her hand in his and smiled.

Broca willed the guardsmen to let Heath free. He went to Alor and Broca said contemptuously. "Get out of my sight."

They went together across the crowded place, toward the archway through which Heath had entered. Still there was silence and no one moved.

The Moon That Vanished

As they reached the archway it vanished, becoming solid wall. Behind them Broca laughed and suddenly the company burst also into wild jeering laughter.

Heath caught Alor tighter by the hand and led her toward another door. It, too, disappeared and the mocking laughter screamed and echoed from the vault.

Broca shouted, "Did you think that I would let you go—you two who betrayed me when I was a man? Even a god can remember!"

Heath saw that the guardsmen and the others were closing in, and he saw how their eyes gleamed. He was filled with a black fear and he put Alor behind him.

Broca cried. "Weakling! Even to save your life, you can't create!"

It was true. He dared not. The shadow-people drew in upon him with their soulless eyes and their faces that were mirrors of the urge to kill.

And then, suddenly, the answer came. Heath's answer rang back. "I will not create—*but I will destroy!*"

Once again he threw the strength of his mind against the Moonfire but this time there was no unhealthy lure to what he did. There was no desire in him but his love for Alor and the need to keep her safe.

The hands of the shadow-people reached out and dragged him away from Alor. He heard her scream and he knew that if he failed they would both be torn to pieces. He summoned all the force that was in him, all the love.

He saw the faces of the shadow-people grow distorted and blurred. He felt their grip weaken and suddenly they were only shadows, a dim multitude in a crumbling castle of dreams.

Broca's goddess faded with the dragon throne and Broca's kingly harness was only a web of memories half-seen above the plain leather.

Broca leaped to his feet with a wild, hoarse cry.

Heath could feel how their two minds locked and swayed on that strange battleground. And as Broca fought to hold his vision, willing the particles of energy into the semblance of matter, so Heath fought to tear them down, to disperse them. For a time the shadows held in that half-world between existence and nothingness.

Then the walls of the castle wavered and ran like red water and were gone. The goddess Alor, the dancers and the slaves and the chieftains, all were gone, and there were only the golden fog and a tall barbarian, stripped of his dreams, and the man Heath and the woman Alor.

Heath looked at Broca and said, "I am stronger than you, because I threw away my godhead."

Broca panted, "I will build again!"

Heath said, "Build."

And he did, his eyes blazing, his massive body shaken with the force of his will. It was all there again, the castle and the multitude of feasters and the jewels.

Broca screamed to his shadow-people. "*Kill!*"

But again, as their hands reached out to destroy, they began to weaken and fade.

Heath cried, "If you want your kingdom, Broca, let us go!"

The castle was now no more than a ghostly outline. Broca's face was beaded with sweat. His hands clawed the air. He swayed with his terrible effort but Heath's dark eyes were bleak and stern. If he had now the look of a god it was a god as ruthless and unshakeable as fate.

The vision crumbled and vanished.

Broca's head dropped. He would not look at them from the bitterness of his defeat. "Get out," he whispered. "Go and let Vakor greet you."

Heath said, "It will be a cleaner death than this."

Alor took his hand and they walked away together through the golden mist. They turned once to look back and already the castle walls were built again, towering magnificent.

"He'll be happy," Heath said, "until he dies."

Alor shuddered. "Let us go."

They went together, away from the pulsing heart of the Moonfire, past the slopes of the crater and down the long way to the harbor. Finally they were aboard the *Ethne* once again.

As they found their slow way out through the island maze Heath held Alor in his arms. They did not speak. Their lips met often with the poignancy of kisses that will not be for long. The golden mists thinned and the fire faded in their blood and the heady sense of power was gone but they did not know nor care.

They came at last out of the veil of the Moonfire and saw ahead the green sail of the *Lahal*, where Vakor waited.

Alor whispered, "Good bye, my love, my David!" and left the bitterness of her tears upon his mouth.

*

The two ships lay side by side in the still water. Vakor was waiting as Heath and Alor came aboard with the other Children of the Moon beside him. He motioned to the seamen who stood there also and said, "Seize them."

But the men were afraid and would not touch them.

Heath saw their faces and wondered. Then, as he looked at Alor, he realized that she was not as she had been before. There was something clean and shining about her now, a new depth and a new calm strength, and in her eyes a strange new beauty. He knew that he himself had changed. They were no longer gods, he and Alor, but they had bathed in the Moonfire and they would never again be quite the same.

He met Vakor's gaze and was not afraid.

The cruel, wolfish face of the priest lost some of its assurance. A queer look of doubt crossed over it.

He said, "Where is Broca?"

"We left him there, building empires in the mist."

"At the heart of the Moonfire?"

"Yes."

"You lie!" cried Vakor. "You could not have come back yourselves, from the heart of the sleeping god. No one ever has." But still the doubt was there.

Heath shrugged. "It doesn't really matter," he said, "whether you believe or not."

There was a long, strange silence. Then the four tall priests in their black tunics said to Vakor, "We must believe. Look into their eyes."

With a solemn ritual gesture they stepped back and left Vakor alone.

Vakor whispered, "It can't be true. The law, the tabu is built on that rock. Men will come out of the fringe as you did, Heath, wrecked and cursed by their blasphemy. But not from the Moonfire itself. Never! That is why the law was made, lest all of Venus die in dreams."

Alor said quietly, "All those others wanted power. We wanted only love. We needed nothing else."

Again there was silence while Vakor stared at them and struggled with himself. Then, very slowly, he said, "You are beyond my power. The sleeping god received you and has chosen to let you go unscathed. I am only a Child of the Moon. I may not judge."

He covered his face and turned away.

One of the lesser priests spoke to Johor. "Let them be given men for their oars."

And Heath and Alor understood that they were free.

Weeks later, Heath and Alor stood at dawn on the shore of the Sea of Morning Opals. The breeze was strong off the land. It filled the golden sail of the *Ethne*, sc that she strained at her mooring lines, eager to be free.

Heath bent and cast them off.

They stood together silently and watched as the little ship gathered speed, going lightly, sweetly and alone into the glory of the morning. The ivory image that was her figurehead lifted its arms to the dawn and smiled and Heath waited there until the last bright gleam of the sail was lost and with it the last of his old life, his memories and his dreams.

Alor touched him gently. He turned and took her in his arms, and they walked away under the *liha*-trees, while the young day brightened in the sky. And they thought how the light of the sun they never saw was more beautiful and full of promise than all the naked wonder of the Moonfire that they had held within their hands.

www.ingramcontent.com/pod-product-compliance
Lightning Source LLC
Chambersburg PA
CBHW021005150626
46549CB00012BA/1315